W9-ACX-243

Cemetery Quilt

Cemetery Quilt

Kent and Alice Ross *Illustrated by* Rosanne Kaloustian

Houghton Mifflin Company Boston 1995

For Mamaw Ross and Mammy Duncan —A.R. and K.R.
For Lisa and Louise with thanks —R.K.

Library of Congress Cataloging-in-Publication Data

Ross, Kent.
Cemetery quilt / by Kent and Alice Ross ; illustrated by Rosanne Kaloustian.
p. cm.
Summary: When her Papaw dies, Josie doesn't want to go to his funeral until her Granny shares with her the family's cemetery quilt.
ISBN 0-395-70948-2
[1. Death—Fiction. 2. Quilts—Fiction. 3. Grandmothers—Fiction.] I. Ross, Alice. II. Kaloustian, Rosanne, ill. III. Title.
PZ7.R719694Ce 1995 94-17617
[E]—dc20 CIP
AC

Printed in the United States of America

HOR 10 9 8 7 6 5 4 3 2 1

Josie was doing the last thing in the world she wanted. She was going to a funeral. And not just any funeral. Her Papaw's. Papaw Henderson.

Josie scrunched deeper into the corner of the back seat. She knew from TV that funerals meant crying and black clothes. And she remembered burying her cat in the back yard after he died. Josie couldn't bear to see another dead body . . . especially not Papaw's.

She scooted forward. "Mom, you know the blue dress you laid out for me? Well . . . I didn't put it in. I packed my red dress."

Her mother sighed. "Josie May, you did that on purpose,

didn't you? Well, it won't keep you from attending the funeral. You'll just have to go in your red dress and look out of place. Someday you'll learn to do what I say."

Josie pressed her cheek to the cold glass. The countryside raced by, gray and colorless. Then she remembered the Red River. Today of all days, Granny would want Josie to see it. She'd say, "That water *is* red, Josie. Not red like a crayon or an apple, but as red as God could make a river."

But Josie couldn't concentrate. She kept thinking of Papaw. Her fingers curled around something in her pocket. A stick of gum.

Papaw had always hidden a piece of gum on the porch. He would tell her "hot" or "cold" until she found it. The last two times Josie had felt silly playing the game. She was too big, but she hadn't been able to tell Papaw. Now she wouldn't need to. To keep from crying, Josie laid her head back and closed her eyes.

She woke to the rock and sway of the car turning into Granny's driveway. "Darn," she thought, "I missed seeing the river!" She heaved open the car door and ran to Granny, plunging her head into the soft rolls of her grandmother's body, inhaling the familiar snuff and butter smell.

"Ya'll have a good trip?" asked Granny.

"I slept some." Josie hoped she wouldn't ask about the river.

"Well the Lord surely gave you his grace of weather."

Entering the house, Josie smelled fried chicken and pumpkin pie. Pumpkin was her favorite. After supper, the grownups talked for a long time. Finally, her mother said, "Why don't you go on to bed, sweetie? You can fix yourself a pallet in Granny's room."

Josie dragged three moth-ball smelling quilts from the closet. One was dark and ugly. She unfolded it on the floor beside the iron bed.

"Oh Lordy, the cemetery quilt," Granny said from the doorway. "I'd near forgot." Her voice was shaky and angry-sounding.

"I'm sorry, Granny. I can put it back," said Josie.

"No, no, I guess it's time you learned about it anyway."

Together they spread out the quilt.

It was ugly. Really ugly.

It ran with smeary mud colors, all brown and gray and rusty. A large square yawned in the center, and inside the square and along the edges of the quilt were small rectangles.

In each rectangle a name was sewn in cursive. Josie read them: Minnie, Opal, Ebenezer . . . They sounded old, yet strangely familiar. Where had she heard those names?

Granny rubbed a finger over the stitching. "My grandma Opal made this quilt in Springfield, Missouri, back in 1829. It's a cemetery quilt. These little patches with names on them are coffins . . ."

"Coffins?"

"Yes. Opal had two boys who died young. She was so heartbroke she made a quilt out of their shirts to remember them by. Made two little coffins and sewed their names on them. Then she quilted them into the center square, like in a cemetery."

"That's terrible, Granny," said Josie, "Like something Dracula would do!"

"No, Josie May, not terrible, just a grievin' thing. Later she made everyone in the family a coffin. When each person died, she'd take their coffin off the border and stitch it into the center —into the cemetery."

“If this was in my closet, I’d have nightmares! Why do you keep it, Granny?”

“Because it’s a family quilt. Our family. See?”

Granny pointed. The name Edward Henderson stared up at Josie. Papaw!

Her heart began to beat faster. She searched the quilt, fearing what she would find.

"I've seen a lot of death in my days . . . ," Granny was saying.

The quilt patterns seemed to spin. Frank Henderson. Her dad.

"Don't know what I'll do without Ed . . ."

Josie felt hot. Why did everyone have to die?

"Haven't worked on the quilt since my brother died, so your name isn't on it yet."

Josie stepped back. "I don't want to be on that quilt! And I don't want to go to any funeral, either!"

But she *did* go to the funeral. In her red dress. No one seemed to notice after all.

From the front pew, Josie glanced at the coffin. She didn't want to look at it. Instead, she studied the walls, trying to find where the music was coming from.

The preacher spoke. He said what a good man Edward Henderson had been. When he finished, he waited by the casket as the people walked by.

"I don't have to see him," Josie told herself. *"They can't make me."*

When their turn came, Granny went forward, but Josie stayed back, watching. Granny's shoulders shook and her sobs echoed through the church.

Josie shut her eyes. She wanted to run, but her feet felt glued to the carpet.

Then Granny walked over and caught her hand. "Don't be afraid," she said. "It's just Papaw's body. Papaw's in another place. A better place."

Josie took one step, then another. Before she knew it, she was looking into the coffin. Granny was right. It looked like Papaw, but it wasn't him. He was gone.

That evening Josie turned the doorknob on the bedroom door.

"Are you moving Papaw to the cemetery?" Josie whispered.

"Trying to, Josie. Been a day, though. Don't know if I can rip a seam."

Granny's hand shook, hovering over the cloth coffin. She popped a stitch and grunted. Popped a stitch and grunted.

"The funeral wasn't so bad," Josie said.

Granny nodded and laid the loose cloth in the center square, carefully setting it right. She fluffed out the quilt and sewed.

Josie watched the crooked fingers move over and under the quilt, sealing the coffin in its new place. Neither spoke.

When the last stitch was in, Josie asked, "Granny, can I be on the quilt?"

"You're family, aren't you? Look in that sack." The sack was full of cloth scraps, all brown and gray and dark green.

Josie thought for a minute. "I'll be right back, Granny."

"Lord, you are the sweetest thing," Granny cried. She reached out to hug Josie and they sat locked together, Granny's head on Josie's shoulder like a little girl's, Josie feeling old like a granny.

Pushing back her hair, Granny started sewing again. Brown uneven stitches grew around Josie's cloth.

In a low voice, Josie confessed, "I missed the river yesterday, Granny."

"That's all right, child. Lord knows I've seen the Red River enough. I just like for you to see it too."

Josie looked at the strange quilt. It was funny, but she felt good about being on the quilt with Dad, and Grandfather, and Granny . . .

All at once Josie asked, “Granny, who’ll bury you when you die?”

Granny smiled with surprise. “Why, someone who loves a fat ugly old woman, I guess.”